NUTCRACKER AND MOUSE-KING

NUTCRACKER AND MOUSE-KING

TRANSLATED

FROM THE GERMAN OF HOFFMANN,

BY

MRS. ST. SIMON.

GYAN

Published by

Gyan Publishing House
5, Ansari Road
Daryaganj, New Delhi-110002
Phone: 011-47034999, 9811692060
E-mail: books@gyanbooks.com

Distribution Network
gyanbooks.com
India, USA, Canada, UK, Australia

ISBN: 978-81-212-8404-2 (HB)
First Published, 1816

2nd Impression 2024

Printed at: Gyan Press, Delhi.

NUTCRACKER AND MOUSE-KING
Author: E. T. A. HOFFMANN, Translator: MRS. ST. SIMON

NUTCRACKER AND MOUSE-KING.

THE NUT-CRACKER

NUTCRACKER AND MOUSE-KING.

TRANSLATED

FROM THE GERMAN OF HOFFMAN,

BY

MRS. ST. SIMON.

With Illustrations on Wood.

NEW-YORK:
D. APPLETON & COMPANY, 200 BROADWAY.
1853.

NUTCRACKER AND MOUSE-KING.

CHRISTMAS EVE.

DURING the long, long day of the twenty-fourth of December, the children of Doctor Stahlbaum were not permitted to enter the parlor, much less the adjoining drawing-room. Frederic and Maria sat nestled together in a corner of the back chamber; dusky twilight had come on, and they felt quite gloomy and fearful, for, as was commonly the case on this day, no light was brought in to them. Fred, in great secrecy, and in a whisper, informed his little sister (she was only just seven years old), that ever since morning he had heard a rustling and a rattling, and now and then a gentle knocking, in the forbidden chambers. Not long ago also he had seen a little dark man, with a large chest under his arm, gliding softly through the entry, but he knew very well that it was nobody but Godfather Drosselmeier. Upon this Maria clapped her little hands together for joy, and exclaimed, "Ah, what beautiful things has Godfather Drosselmeier made for us this time!"

Counsellor Drosselmeier was not a very handsome man; he was small and thin, had many wrinkles in his face, over his right eye he had a large black patch, and he was without hair, for which reason he wore a very nice white wig; this was made of glass however, and was a very ingenious piece of work. The Godfather himself was very ingenious also, he understood all about clocks and watches, and could even make them. Accordingly, when any one of the beautiful clocks in Doctor Stahlbaum's house was sick, and could not sing, Godfather Drosselmeier would have to attend it. He would then take off his glass wig, pull off his brown coat, put on a blue apron, and pierce the clock with sharp-pointed instruments, which usually caused little Maria a great deal of anxiety. But it did the clock no harm; on the contrary, it became quite lively again, and began at once right merrily to rattle, and to strike, and to sing, so that it was a pleasure to all who heard it. Whenever he came, he always brought something pretty in his pocket for the children, sometimes a little man who moved his eyes and made a bow, at others, a box, from which a little bird hopped out when it was opened—sometimes one thing, sometimes another.

When Christmas Eve came, he had always a beautiful piece of work prepared for them, which had cost him a great deal of trouble, and on this account it was always carefully preserved by their parents, after he had given it to them. "Ah, what beautiful present has Godfather Drosselmeier made for us this time!" exclaimed Maria. It was Fred's opinion that this time it could be nothing else than a castle, in which all kinds of fine soldiers marched up and down and went through their exercises; then other soldiers would come, and try to break into the castle, but the soldiers within would fire off their cannon very bravely, until all roared and cracked again. "No, no," cried Maria, interrupting him, "Godfather Drosselmeier has told me of a lovely garden where there is a great lake, upon which beautiful swans swim about, with golden collars around their necks, and sing their sweetest songs. Then there comes a little girl out of the garden down along the lake, and coaxes the swans to the shore, and feeds them with sweet cake."

"Swans never eat cake," interrupted Fred, somewhat roughly, "and even Godfather Drosselmeier himself can't make a whole garden. After all, we have little good of his playthings; they are all taken right away from us again. I like what Papa and Mamma give us much better, for we can keep their presents for ourselves, and do as we please with them." The children now began once more to guess what it could be this time. Maria thought that Miss Trutchen (her great doll) was growing very old, for she fell almost every moment upon the floor, and more awkwardly than ever, which could not happen without leaving sad marks upon her face, and as to neatness in dress, this was now altogether out of the question with her. Scolding did not help the matter in the least. Frederic declared, on the other hand, that a bay horse was wanting in his stable, and his troops were very deficient in cavalry, as his Papa very well knew.

By this time it had become quite dark. Frederic and Maria sat close together, and did not venture again to speak a word. It seemed now as if soft wings rustled around them, and very distant, but sweet music was heard at intervals. At this moment a shrill sound broke upon their ears—kling, ling—kling, ling—the doors flew wide open, and such a dazzling light broke out from the great chamber, that with the loud exclamation, "Ah! ah!" the children stood fixed at the threshold. But Papa and Mamma stepped to the door, took them by the hand, and said, "Come, come, dear children, and see what Christmas has brought you this year."

THE GIFTS.

Kind reader, or listener, whatever may be your name, whether Frank, Robert, Henry,—Anna or Maria, I beg you to call to mind the table covered with your last Christmas gifts, as in their newest gloss they first appeared to your delighted vision. You will then be able to imagine the astonishment of the children, as they stood with sparkling eyes, unable to utter a word, for joy at the sight before them. At last Maria called out with a deep sigh, "Ah, how beautiful! ah, how beautiful!" and Frederic gave two or three leaps in the air higher than he had ever done before. The children must have been very obedient and good children during the past year, for never on any Christmas Eve before, had so many beautiful things been given to them. A tall Fir tree stood in the middle of the room, covered with gold and silver apples, while sugar almonds, comfits, lemon drops, and every kind of confectionery, hung like buds and blossoms upon all its branches. But the greatest beauty about this wonderful tree, was the many little lights that sparkled amid its dark boughs, which like stars illuminated its treasures, or like friendly eyes seemed to invite the children to partake of its blossoms and fruit.

The table under the tree shone and flushed with a thousand different colors—ah, what beautiful things were there! who can describe them? Maria spied the prettiest dolls, a tea set, all kinds of nice little furniture, and what eclipsed all the rest, a silk dress tastefully ornamented with gay ribbons, which hung upon a frame before her eyes, so that she could view it on every side. This she did too, and exclaimed over and over again, "Ah, the sweet—ah, the dear, dear frock! and may I put it on? yes, yes —may I really, though, wear it?"

In the meanwhile Fred had been galloping round and round the room, trying his new bay horse, which, true enough, he had found, fastened by its bridle to the table. Dismounting again, he said it was a wild creature, but that was nothing; he would soon break him. He then reviewed his new regiment of hussars, who were very elegantly arrayed in red and gold, and carried silver weapons, and rode upon such bright shining horses, that you would almost believe these were of pure silver also. The children had now become somewhat more composed, and turned to the picture books, which lay open on the table, where all kinds of beautiful flowers, and gayly dressed people, and boys and girls at play, were painted as natural as if they were alive. Yes, the children had just turned to these singular books, when—kling, ling, kling, ling—the bell was heard again. They knew that Godfather Drosselmeier was now about to display his Christmas gift, and ran towards a table that stood against the wall, covered by a curtain reaching from the ceiling to the floor. The curtain behind which he had remained so long concealed, was quickly drawn aside, and what saw the children then?

Upon a green meadow, spangled with flowers, stood a noble castle, with clear glass windows and golden turrets. A musical clock began to play, when the doors and windows flew open, and little men and women, with feathers in their hats, and long flowing trains, were seen sauntering about in the rooms. In the middle hall, which seemed as if it were all on fire, so many little tapers were burning in silver chandeliers, there were children in white frocks and green jackets, dancing to the sound of the music. A man in an emerald-green cloak, at intervals put his head out of the window, nodded, and then disappeared; and Godfather Drosselmeier himself, only that he was not much bigger than Papa's thumb, came now and then to the door of the castle, looked about him, and then went in again. Fred, with his arms resting upon the table, gazed at the beautiful castle, and the little walking and dancing figures, and then said, "Godfather Drosselmeier, let me go into your castle."

The Counsellor gave him to understand that that could not be done. And he was right, for it was foolish in Fred to wish to go into a castle, which with all its golden turrets was not as high as his head. Fred saw that likewise himself. After a while as the men and women kept walking back and forth, and the children danced, and the emerald man looked out at his window, and Godfather Drosselmeier came to the door, and all without the least change; Fred called out impatiently, "Godfather Drosselmeier, come out this time at the other door."

"That can never be, dear Fred," said the Counsellor.

"Well then," continued Frederic, "let the green man who peeps out at the window walk about with the rest."

"And that can never be," rejoined the Counsellor.

"Then the children must come down," cried Fred, "I want to see them nearer."

"All that can never be, I say," replied the Counsellor, a little out of humor. "As the mechanism is made, so it must remain."

"So——o," cried Fred, in a drawling tone, "all that can never be! Listen, Godfather Drosselmeier. If your little dressed up figures in the castle there, can do nothing else but always the same thing, they are not good for much, and I care very little about them. No, give me my hussars, who can manœuvre backward and forward, as I order them, and are not shut up in a house."

With this, he darted towards a large table, drew up his regiment upon their silver horses, and let them trot and gallop, and cut and slash, to his heart's content. Maria also had softly stolen away, for she too was soon tired of the sauntering and dancing puppets in the castle; but as she was very amiable and good, she did not wish it to be observed so plainly in her as it was in her brother Fred. Counsellor Drosselmeier turned to the parents, and said, somewhat angrily, "An ingenious work like this was not made for stupid children. I will put up my castle again, and carry it home." But their mother now stepped forward, and desired to see the secret mechanism and curious works by which the little figures were set in motion. The Counsellor took it all apart, and then put it together again. While he was employed in this manner he became good-natured once more, and gave the children some nice brown men and women, with gilt faces, hands, and feet. They were all made of sweet thorn, and smelt like gingerbread, at which Frederic and Maria were greatly delighted. At her mother's request, the elder sister, Louise, had put on the new dress which had been given to her, and she looked most charmingly in it, but Maria, when it came to her turn, thought she would like to look at hers a while longer as it hung. This was readily permitted.

THE FAVORITE.

The truth is, Maria was unwilling to leave the table then, because she had discovered something upon it, which no one had yet remarked. By the marching out of Fred's hussars, who had been drawn up close to the tree, a curious little man came into view, who stood there silent and retired, as if he were waiting quietly for his turn to be noticed. It must be confessed, a great deal could not be said in favor of the beauty of his figure, for not only was his rather broad, stout body, out of all proportion to the little, slim legs that carried it, but his head was by far too large for either. A genteel dress went a great way to compensate for these defects, and led to the belief that he must be a man of taste and good breeding. He wore a hussar's jacket of beautiful bright violet, fastened together with white loops and buttons, pantaloons of exactly the same color, and the neatest boots that ever graced the foot of a student or an officer. They fitted as tight to his little legs as if they were painted upon them. It was laughable to see, that in addition to this handsome apparel, he had hung upon his back a narrow clumsy cloak, that looked as if it were made of wood, and upon his head he wore a woodman's cap; but Maria remembered that Godfather Drosselmeier wore an old shabby cloak and an ugly cap, and still he was a dear, dear godfather. Maria could not help thinking also, that even if Godfather Drosselmeier were in other respects as well dressed as this little fellow, yet after all he would not look half so handsome as he. The longer Maria gazed upon the little man whom she had taken a liking to at first sight, the more she was sensible how much good nature and friendliness was expressed in his features. Nothing but kindness and benevolence shone in his clear green, though somewhat too prominent eyes. It was very becoming to the man that he wore about his chin a nicely trimmed beard of white cotton, for by this the sweet smile upon his deep red lips was rendered much more striking. "Ah, dear father," exclaimed Maria at last, "to whom belongs that charming little man by the tree there?"

"He shall work industriously for you all, dear child," said her father. "He can crack the hardest nuts with his teeth, and he belongs as well to Louise as to you and Fred." With these words her father took him carefully from the table, and raised up his wooden cloak, whereupon the little man stretched his mouth wide open, and showed two rows of very white sharp teeth. At her father's bidding Maria put in a nut, and—crack—the man had bitten it in two, so that the shell fell off, and Maria caught the sweet kernel in her hand. Maria and the other two children were now informed that this dainty little man came of the family of Nutcrackers, and practised the profession of his forefathers. Maria was overjoyed at what she heard, and her father said, "Dear Maria, since friend Nutcracker is so great a favorite with you, I place him under your particular care and keeping, although, as I said before, Louise and Fred shall have as much right to his services as you."

Maria took him immediately in her arms, and set him to cracking nuts, but she picked out the smallest, that the little fellow need not stretch his mouth open so wide, which in truth was not very becoming to him. Louise sat down by her, and friend Nutcracker must perform the same service for her too, which he seemed to do quite willingly, for he kept smiling all the while very pleasantly. In the mean time Fred had become tired of riding and parading his hussars, and when he heard the nuts crack so merrily, he ran to his sister, and laughed very heartily at the droll little man, who now, since Fred must have a share in the sport, passed from hand to hand, and thus there was no end to his labor. Fred always chose the biggest and hardest nuts, when all at once—crack—crack—it went, and three teeth fell out of Nutcracker's mouth, and his whole under jaw became loose and rickety. "Ah, my poor dear Nutcracker!" said Maria, and snatched him out of Fred's hands.

"That's a stupid fellow," said Fred. "He wants to be a nutcracker, and has poor teeth—he don't understand his trade. Give him to me, Maria. He shall crack nuts for me if he loses all his teeth, and his whole chin into the bargain. Why make such a fuss about such a fellow?"

"No, no," exclaimed Maria, weeping; "you shall not have my dear Nutcracker. See how sorrowfully he looks at me, and shows me his poor mouth. But you are a hard-hearted fellow; you beat your horses; yes, and lately you had one of your soldiers shot through the head."

"That's all right," said Fred, "though you don't understand it. But Nutcracker belongs as much to me as to you, so let me have him."

Maria began to cry bitterly, and rolled up the sick Nutcracker as quickly as she could in her little pocket handkerchief. Their parents now came up with Godfather Drosselmeier. The latter, to Maria's great distress, took Fred's part. But their father said, "I have placed Nutcracker expressly under Maria's protection, and as I see that he is now greatly in need of it, I give her full authority over him, and no one must dispute it. Besides, I wonder at Fred, that he should require farther duty from one who has been maimed in the service. As a good soldier, he ought to know that the wounded are not expected to take their place in the ranks."

Fred was much ashamed, and without troubling himself farther about nuts or Nutcracker, stole around to the opposite end of the table, where his hussars, after stationing suitable outposts, had encamped for the night. Maria collected together Nutcracker's lost teeth, tied up his wounded chin with a nice white ribbon which she had taken from her dress, and then wrapped up the little fellow more carefully than ever in her handkerchief, for he looked very pale and frightened. Thus she held him, rocking him in her arms like a little child, while she looked over the beautiful pictures of the new picture-book, which she found among her other Christmas gifts. Contrary to her usual disposition, she showed some ill-temper towards Father Drosselmeier, who kept continually laughing at her, and asked again and again how it was that she liked to caress such an ugly little fellow. That singular comparison with Drosselmeier, which she made when her eyes first fell upon Nutcracker, now came again into her mind, and she said very seriously: "Who knows, dear godfather, if you were dressed like my sweet Nutcracker, and had on such bright little boots—who knows but you would then be as handsome as he is?" Maria could not tell why her parents laughed so loudly at this, and why the Counsellor's face turned so red, and he, for his part, did not laugh half so heartily this time as he had done more than once before. It is likely there was some particular reason for it.

WONDERS UPON WONDERS.

In the sitting-room of the Doctor's house, just as you enter the room, there stands on the left hand, close against the wall, a high glass-case, in which the children preserve all the beautiful things which are given to them every year. Louise was quite a little girl when her father had the case made by a skilful joiner, who set in it such large, clear panes of glass, and arranged all the parts so well together, that every thing looked much brighter and handsomer when on its shelves than when it was held in the hands. On the upper shelf, which Maria and Fred were unable to reach, stood all Godfather Drosselmeier's curious machines. Immediately below this was a shelf for the picture-books; the two lower shelves Maria and Fred filled up as they pleased, but it always happened that Maria used the lower one as a house for her dolls, while Fred, on the contrary, cantoned his troops in the one above.

And so it happened to-day, for while Fred set his hussars in order above, Maria, having laid Miss Trutchen aside, and having installed the new and sweetly dressed doll in her best furnished chamber below, had invited herself to tea with her. I have said that the chamber was well furnished, and it is true; here was a nice chintz sofa and several tiny chairs, there stood a tea-table, but above all, there was a clean, white little bed for her doll to repose upon. All these things were arranged in one corner of the glass case, the sides of which were hung with gay pictures, and it will readily be supposed, that in such a chamber the new doll, Miss Clara, must have found herself very comfortable.

It was now late in the evening, and night, indeed, was close at hand, and Godfather Drosselmeier had long since gone home, yet still the children could not leave the glass-case, although their mother repeatedly told them that it was high time to go to bed. "It is true," cried Fred at last; "the poor fellows (meaning his hussars) would like to get a little rest, and as long as I am here, not one of them will dare to nod—I know that." With these words he went up to bed, but Maria begged very hard, "Only leave me here a little while, dear mother. I have two or three things to attend to, and when they are done I will go immediately to bed." Maria was a very good and sensible child, and therefore her mother could leave her alone with her playthings without anxiety. But for fear she might become so much interested in her new doll and other presents as to forget the lights which burned around the glass case, her mother blew them all out, and left only the lamp which hung down from the ceiling in the middle of the chamber, and which diffused a soft, pleasant light. "Come in soon, dear Maria, or you will not be up in time to-morrow morning," called her mother, as she went up to bed. There was something Maria had at heart to do, which she had not told her mother, though she knew not the reason why; and as soon as she found herself alone she went quickly about it. She still carried in her arms the wounded Nutcracker, rolled up in her pocket handkerchief. Now she laid him carefully upon the table, unrolled the handkerchief softly, and examined his wound. Nutcracker was very pale, but still he smiled so kindly and sorrowfully that it went straight to Maria's heart. "Ah! Nutcracker, Nutcracker, do not be angry at brother Fred because he hurt you so, he did not mean to be so rough; it is the wild soldier's life with his hussars that has made him a little hard-hearted, but otherwise he is a good fellow, I can assure you. Now I will tend you very carefully until you are well and merry again; as to fastening in your teeth and setting your shoulders, that Godfather Drosselmeier must do; he understands such things."

But Maria was hardly able to finish the sentence, for as she mentioned the name of Drosselmeier, friend Nutcracker made a terrible wry face, and there darted something out of his eyes like green sparkling flashes. Maria was just going to fall into a dreadful fright, when behold, it was the sad smiling face of the honest Nutcracker again, which she saw before her, and she knew now that it must be the glare of the lamp, which, stirred by the draught, had flared up, and distorted Nutcracker's features so strangely. "Am I not a foolish girl," she said, "to be so easily frightened, and to think that a wooden puppet could make faces at me? But I love Nutcracker too well, because he is so droll and so good tempered; therefore he shall be taken good care of as he deserves." With this

Maria took friend Nutcracker in her arms, walked to the glass case, stooped down, and said to her new doll, "Pray, Miss Clara, be so good as to give up your bed to the sick and wounded Nutcracker, and make out as well as you can with the sofa. Remember that you are well and hearty, or you would not have such fat red cheeks, and very few little dolls have such nice sofas."

Miss Clara, in her gay Christmas attire, looked very grand and haughty, and would not even say "Muck." "But why should I stand upon ceremony?" said Maria, and she took out the bed, laid little Nutcracker down upon it softly, and gently rolled a nice ribbon which she wore around her waist, about his poor shoulders, and then drew the bedclothes over him snugly, so that there was nothing to be seen of him below the nose. "He shan't stay with the naughty Clara," she said, and raised the bed with Nutcracker in it to the shelf above, and placed it close by the pretty village, where Fred's hussars were quartered. She locked the case, and was about to go up to bed, when—listen children—when softly, softly it began to rustle, and to whisper, and to rattle round and round, under the hearth, behind the chairs, behind the cupboards and glass case. The great clock whirred louder and louder, but it could not strike. Maria turned towards it, and there the large gilt owl that sat on the top, had dropped down its wings, so that they covered the whole face, and it stretched out its ugly head with the short crooked beak, and looked just like a cat. And the clock whirred louder in plain words. "Dick—ry, dick—ry, dock—whirr, softly clock, Mouse-King has a fine ear—prr—prr—pum—pum—the old song let him hear—prr—prr—pum—pum—or he might—run away in a fright—now clock strike softly and light." And pum—pum, it went with a dull deadened sound twelve times. Maria began now to tremble with fear, and she was upon the point of running out of the room in terror, when she beheld Godfather Drosselmeier, who sat in the owl's place on the top of the clock, and had hung down the skirts of his brown coat just like wings. But she took courage, and cried out loudly, with sobs, "Godfather Drosselmeier, Godfather Drosselmeier, what are you doing up there? Come down, and do not frighten me so, you naughty Godfather Drosselmeier!"

Just then a wild squeaking and whimpering broke out on all sides, and then there was a running, trotting and galloping behind the walls, as if a thousand little feet were in motion, and a thousand little lights flashed out of the crevices in the floor. But they were not lights—no—they were sparkling little eyes, and Maria perceived that mice were all around, peeping out and working their way into the room. Presently it went trot—trot—hop—hop about the chamber, and more and more mice, in greater or smaller parties galloped across, and at last placed themselves in line and column, just as Fred was accustomed to place his soldiers when they went to battle. This Maria thought was very droll, and as she had not that aversion to mice which most children have, her terror was gradually leaving her, when all at once there arose a squeaking so terrible and piercing, that it seemed as if ice-cold water was poured down her back. Ah, what now did she see!

I know, my worthy reader Frederic, that thy heart, like that of the wise and brave soldier Frederic Stahlbaum, sits in the right place, but if thou hadst seen what Maria now beheld, thou wouldst certainly have run away; yes, I believe that thou wouldst have jumped as quickly as possible into bed, and then have drawn the covering over thine ears much farther than was necessary to keep thee warm. Alas! poor Maria could not do that now, for—listen children—close before her feet, there burst out sand and lime and crumbled wall stones, as if thrown up by some subterranean force, and seven mice-heads with seven sparkling crowns rose out of the floor, sqeaking and squealing terribly. Presently the mouse's body to which these seven heads belonged, worked its way out, and the great mouse crowned with the seven diadems, squeaking loudly, huzzaed in full chorus, as he advanced to meet his army, which at once set itself in motion, and hott—hott—trot—trot it went—alas, straight towards the glass case—straight towards poor Maria who stood close before it!

Her heart had before beat so terribly from anxiety and fear, that she thought it would leap out of her bosom, and then she knew she must die; but now it seemed as if the blood stood still in her veins. Half fainting, she tottered backward, when clatter—clatter—rattle—rattle it went—and a glass pane which she had struck with her elbow fell in pieces at her feet. She felt at the moment a sharp pain in her left arm, but her heart all at once became much lighter, she heard no more squeaking and squealing, all had become still, and although she did not dare to look, yet she believed that the mice, frightened by the clatter of the broken glass, had retreated into their holes. But what was that again! Close behind her in the glass case a strange bustling and rustling began, and little fine voices were heard. "Up, up, awake—arms take—awake—to the fight—this night—up, up—to the fight." And all the while something rang out clear and sweet like little bells. "Ah, that is my dear musical clock!" exclaimed Maria joyfully, and turned quickly to look.

She then saw how it flashed and lightened strangely in the glass case, and there was a great stir and bustle upon the shelves. Many little figures crossed up and down by each other, and worked and stretched out their arms as if they were making ready. And now, Nutcracker raised himself all of a sudden, threw the bed-clothes clear off, and leaped with both feet at once out of bed, crying aloud, "Crack—crack—crack—stupid pack—drive mouse back—stupid pack—crack—crack—mouse—back—crick—crack—stupid pack." With these words he drew his little sword, flourished it in the air, and exclaimed, "My loving vassals, friends and brothers, will you stand by me in the hard fight?" Straightway three Scaramouches, a Harlequin, four Chimney-sweepers, two Guitar-players and a drummer cried out, "Yes, my lord, we will follow you with fidelity and courage—we will march with you to battle—to victory or death," and then rushed after the fiery Nutcracker, who ventured the dangerous leap down from the upper shelf. Ah, it was easy enough for *them* to perform this feat, for beside the fine garments of thick cloth and silk which they wore, the inside of their bodies were made of cotton and tow, so that they came down plump, like bags of wool. But poor Nutcracker had certainly broken his arms or his legs, for remember, it was almost two feet from the shelf where he stood to the floor, and his body was as brittle as if it had been cut out of Linden wood. Yes, Nutcracker would certainly have broken his arms or his legs, if, at the moment when he leaped, Miss Clara had not sprung quickly from the sofa, and caught the hero with his drawn sword in her soft arms. "Ah, thou dear, good Clara," sobbed Maria, "how I have wronged thee! Thou didst certainly resign thy bed willingly to little Nutcracker."

But Miss Clara now spoke, as she softly pressed the young hero to her silken bosom. "You will not, oh, my lord! sick and wounded as you are, share the dangers of the fight. See how your brave vassals assemble themselves, eager for the affray, and certain of conquest. Scaramouch, Harlequin, Chimney-sweepers, Guitar-players, Drummer, are all ready drawn up below, and the china figures on the shelf stir and move strangely! Will you not, oh, my lord! repose upon the sofa, or from my arms look down upon your victory?" Thus spoke Clara, but Nutcracker demeaned himself very ungraciously, for he kicked and struggled so violently with his legs, that Clara was obliged to set him quickly down upon the floor. He then, however, dropped gracefully upon one knee, and said, "Fair lady, the recollection of thy favor and condescension will go with me into the battle and the strife."

Clara then stooped so low that she could take him by the arm, raised him gently from his knees, took off her bespangled girdle, and was about to throw it across his neck, but little Nutcracker stepped two paces backward, laid his hand upon his breast, and said very earnestly, "Not so, fair lady, lavish not thy favors thus upon me, for—" he stopped, sighed heavily, tore off the ribbon which Maria had bound about his shoulders, pressed it to his lips, hung it across him like a scarf, and then boldly flourishing his bright little blade, leaped like a bird over the edge of the glass case upon the floor. You understand my kind and good readers and listeners, that Nutcracker, even before he had thus come to life, had felt very sensibly the kindness and love which Maria had shown towards him, and it was because he had become so partial to her, that he would not receive and wear the girdle of Miss Clara, although it shone and sparkled so brightly. The true and faithful Nutcracker preferred to wear Maria's simple ribbon. But what will now happen? As soon as Nutcracker had leaped out, the squeaking and whistling was heard again. Ah, it is under the large table, that the hateful mice have concealed their countless bands, and high above them all towers the dreadful mouse with seven heads! What will now happen!

THE BATTLE.

"Beat the march, true vassal Drummer!" screamed Nutcracker very loudly, and immediately the drummer began to rattle and to roll upon his drum so skilfully, that the windows of the glass case trembled and hummed again. Now it rustled and clattered therein, and Maria perceived that the covers of the little boxes in which Fred's army were quartered, were bursting open, and now the soldiers leaped out, and then down again upon the lowest shelf, where they drew up in fine array. Nutcracker ran up and down, speaking inspiring words to the troops —"Let no dog of a trumpeter blow or stir!" he cried angrily, for he was afraid he should not be heard, and then turned quickly to Harlequin, who had grown a little pale, and chattered with his long chin. "General," he said, earnestly, "I know your courage and your experience; there is need now for a quick eye, and skill to seize the proper moment. I intrust to your command all the cavalry and artillery. You do not need a horse, for you have very long legs, and can gallop yourself tolerably well. I look to see you do your duty." Thereupon Harlequin put his long, thin fingers to his mouth, and crowed so piercingly, that it sounded as if a hundred shrill trumpets were blown merrily.

Then it stirred again in the glass case—a neighing, and a whinnying, and a stamping were heard, and see! Fred's cuirassiers and dragoons, but above all, his new splendid hussars marched out, and halted close by the case. Regiment after regiment now defiled before Nutcracker, with flying colors and warlike music, and ranged themselves in long rows across the floor of the chamber. Before them went Fred's cannon rattling along, surrounded by the cannoniers, and soon bom—bom it went, and Maria could see how the mice suffered by the fire, how the sugar-plums plunged into their dark, heavy mass, covering them with white powder, and throwing them more than once into shameful disorder. But the greatest damage was done them by a heavy battery that was mounted upon mamma's footstool, which—pum, pum—kept up a steady fire of caraway seeds against the enemy, by which a great many of them fell. The mice, notwithstanding, came nearer and nearer, and at last mastered some of the cannon, but then it went prr—prr—and Maria could scarcely see what now happened for the smoke and dust. This however was certain, that each corps fought with the greatest animosity, and the victory was for a long time doubtful. The mice kept deploying more and more forces, and the little silver shot, which they fired very skilfully, struck now even into the glass case. Clara and Trutchen ran around in despair. "Must I die in the blossom of youth?" said Clara. "Have I so well preserved myself for this, to perish here in these walls?" cried Trutchen. Then they fell about each other's necks, and screamed so terribly, that they could be heard above the mad tumult of the battle.

Of the scene that now presented itself you can have no idea, good reader. It went prr—prr—puff—piff—clitter—clatter—bom, burum—bom, burum—bom—in the wildest confusion, while the Mouse-King and mice squeaked and screamed, and now and then the mighty voice of Nutcracker was heard, as he gave the necessary orders, and he was seen striding along through the battalions in the hottest of the fire. Harlequin had made some splendid charges with his cavalry, and covered himself with honor, but Fred's hussars were battered by the enemy's artillery, with odious, offensive balls, which made dreadful spots in their red jackets, for which reason they would not move forward. Harlequin ordered them to draw off to the left, and in the enthusiasm of command headed the movement himself, and the cuirassiers and dragoons followed; that is, they all drew off to the left, and galloped home. By this step the battery upon the footstool was exposed to great danger, and it was not long before a strong body of very ugly mice pushed on with such determined bravery, that the footstool, cannons, cannoniers and all were overthrown by their headlong charge. Nutcracker seemed a little disturbed at this, and gave orders that the right wing should make a retreating movement. You know very well, oh my military reader Frederic, that to make such a movement is almost the same thing as to run away, and you are now grieving with me at the disaster which impends over the army of Maria's darling Nutcracker.

But turn your eyes from this scene, and view the left wing, where all is still in good order, and where there is yet great hope, both for the general and the army. During the hottest of the fight, large masses of mice cavalry had debouched softly from under the settee, and amid loud and hideous squeaking had thrown themselves with fury upon the left wing; but what an obstinate resistance did they meet with there! Slowly, as the difficult nature of the ground required—for the edge of the glass case had to be traversed—the china figures had advanced, headed by two Chinese emperors, and formed themselves into a hollow square. These brave, motley, but noble troops, which were composed of Gardeners, Tyrolese, Bonzes, Friseurs, Merry-andrews, Cupids, Lions, Tigers, Peacocks, and Apes, fought with coolness, courage, and determination. By their Spartan bravery this battalion of picked men would have wrested the victory from the foe, had not a bold major rushed madly from the enemy's ranks, and bitten off the head of one of the Chinese emperors, who in falling dashed to the ground two Bonzes and a Cupid. Through this gap the enemy penetrated into the square, and in a few moments the whole battalion was torn to pieces. Their brave resistance, therefore, was of no avail to Nutcracker's army, which, once having begun to retreat, retired farther and farther, and at every step with diminished numbers, until the unfortunate Nutcracker halted with a little band close before the glass case. "Let the reserve advance! Harlequin—Scaramouch—Drummer—where are you?"

Thus cried Nutcracker, in hopes of new troops which should deploy out of the glass-case. And there actually came forth a few brown men and women, made of sweet thorn, with golden faces, and caps, and helmets, but they fought around so awkwardly, that they did not hit one of the enemy, and at last knocked the cap off their own general's head. The enemies' chasseurs, too, bit off their legs before long, so that they tumbled over, and carried with them to the ground some of Nutcracker's best officers. Nutcracker, now completely surrounded by the foe, was in the greatest peril.

He tried to leap over the edge, into the glass case, but found his legs too short. Clara and Trutchen lay each in a deep swoon,—they could not help him—hussars, dragoons sprang merrily by him into safe quarters, and in wild despair, he cried, "A horse—a horse—a kingdom for a horse!" At this moment two of the enemies' tirailleurs seized him by his wooden mantle, and the Mouse-King, squeaking from his seven throats, leaped in triumph towards him. Maria could no longer control herself. "Oh, my poor Nutcracker!" she cried, sobbing, and without being exactly conscious of what she did, grasped her left shoe, and threw it with all her strength into the thickest of the mice, straight at their king. In an instant, all seemed scattered and dispersed, but Maria felt in her left arm a still sharper pain than before, and sank in a swoon to the floor.

THE SICKNESS.

When Maria woke out of her deep and deathlike slumber, she found herself lying in her own bed, with the sun shining bright and sparkling through the ice-covered windows into the chamber. Close beside her sat a stranger, whom she soon recognized, however, as the Surgeon Wendelstern. He said softly, "She is awake!" Her mother then came to the bedside, and gazed upon her with anxious and inquiring looks. "Ah, dear mother," lisped little Maria, "are all the hateful mice gone, and is the good Nutcracker safe?"

"Do not talk such foolish stuff," replied her mother; "what have the mice to do with Nutcracker? You naughty child, you have caused us a great deal of anxiety. But so it always is, when children are disobedient and do not mind their parents. You played last night with your dolls until it was very late. You became sleepy, probably, and a stray mouse may have jumped out and frightened you; at all events, you broke a pane of glass with your elbow, and cut your arm so severely, that neighbor Wendelstern, who has just taken the piece of glass out of the wound, declares that it came very near cutting a vein, in which case you might have had a stiff arm all your life, or perhaps have bled to death. It was fortunate that I woke about midnight, and not finding you in your bed, got up and went into the sitting-room. There you lay in a swoon upon the floor, close by the glass case, the blood flowing in a stream. I almost fainted away myself at the sight. There you lay, and scattered around, were many of Frederic's leaden soldiers, broken China figures, gingerbread men and women and other playthings, and not far off your left shoe."

"Ah! dear mother, dear mother," exclaimed

Maria, interrupting her, "those were the traces of that dreadful battle between the puppets and the mice, and what frightened me so was the danger of poor Nutcracker, when the mice were going to take him prisoner. Then I threw my shoe at the mice, and after that I don't know what happened."

Surgeon Wendelstern here made a sign to the mother, and she said very softly to Maria, "Well, never mind about it, my dear child, the mice are all gone, and little Nutcracker stands safe and sound in the glass case." Doctor Stahlbaum now entered the chamber, and spoke for a while with Surgeon Wendelstern, then he felt Maria's pulse, and she could hear very plainly that he said something about a fever. She was obliged to remain in bed and take physic, and so it continued for some days, although except a slight pain in her arm, she felt quite well and comfortable. She knew little Nutcracker had escaped safe from the battle, and it seemed to her that she sometimes heard his voice quite plainly, as if in a dream, saying mournfully, "Maria, dearest lady, what thanks do I not owe you! but you can do still more for me." Maria tried to think what it could be, but in vain; nothing occurred to her. She could not play very well on account of the wound in her arm, and when she tried to read or look at her picture books, a strange glare came across her eyes, so that she was obliged to desist. The time, during the day, always seemed very long to her, and she waited impatiently for evening, as her mother then usually seated herself by her bedside, and read or related some pretty story to her.

One evening she had just finished the wonderful history of prince Fackardin, when the door opened, and Godfather Drosselmeier entered, saying, "I must see now for myself how it goes with the sick and wounded Maria." As soon as Maria saw Godfather Drosselmeier in his brown coat, the image of that night in which Nutcracker lost the battle against the mice, returned vividly to her mind, and she cried out involuntarily, "Oh Godfather Drosselmeier, you have been very naughty; I saw you as you sat upon the clock, and covered it with your wings, so that it should not strike loud, to scare away the mice. I heard how you called out to the Mouse-King. Why did you not come to help us; me, and the poor Nutcracker? It is all your fault, naughty Godfather Drosselmeier, that I must lie here sick in bed." Her mother was quite frightened at this, and said, "What is the matter with you, dear Maria?"

But Godfather Drosselmeier made very strange faces, and said in a grating, monotonous tone, "Pendulum must whirr—whirr—whirr—this way—that way—clock will strike—tired of ticking—all the day—softly whirr—whirr—whirr—strike kling—klang—strike klang—kling—bing and bang and bang and bing—'twill scare away the Mouse-King. Then Owl in swift flight comes at dead of night. Pendulum must whirr —whirr—Clock will strike kling—klang—this way—that way—tired of ticking all the day—bing — bang — and Mouse-King scare away—whirr—whirr—prr—prr." Maria stared at Godfather Drosselmeier, for he did not look at all as he usually did, but appeared much uglier, and he moved his right arm backward and forward, like a puppet pulled by wires. She would have been afraid of him, if her mother had not been present, and if Fred had not slipped in, in the meanwhile, and interrupted him with loud laughter. "Ha, ha! Godfather Drosselmeier," cried Fred, "you are to-day too droll again—you act just like my Harlequin that I threw into the lumber room long ago." But their mother was very serious, and said, "Dear Counsellor, this is very strange sport—what do you really mean by it?"

"Gracious me," replied Drosselmeier, laughing, "have you forgotten then my pretty watchmaker's song? I always sing it to such patients as Maria." With this he drew his chair close to her bed, and said, "Do not be angry that I did not pick out the Mouse-King's fourteen eyes—that could not be—but instead, I have in store for you a very agreeable surprise." The Counsellor with these words put his hand in his pocket, drew something out slowly, and behold it was—Nutcracker with his lost teeth nicely fastened in, and his lame chin well set and sound. Maria cried aloud with joy, while her mother smiled, and said, "You see now, Maria, that Godfather Drosselmeier meant well by your little Nutcracker."

"But still you must confess," Maria, said the Counsellor, "that Nutcracker's figure is none of the finest, neither can his face be called exactly handsome. How this ugliness came to be hereditary in the family, I will now relate to you, if you will listen. Or perhaps you know already the story of the Princess Pirlipat and the Lady Mouserings, and the skilful Watchmaker?"

"Look here, Godfather Drosselmeier," interrupted Fred, "Nutcracker's teeth you have fastened in very well, and his chin is no longer lame and rickety, but why has he no sword? why have you not put on his sword?"

"Ah," replied the Counsellor, angrily, "you must always meddle and make, you rogue. What is Nutcracker's sword to me? I have cured his wounds, and he may find a sword for himself as he can."

"That's true," said Fred, "he is a brave fellow, and will know how to get one."

"Tell me then, Maria," continued the Counsellor, "have you heard the story of the Princess Pirlipat?"

"I hope, dear Counsellor," said the mother, "that your story will not be frightful, as those that you narrate usually are."

"By no means, dearest madam," replied Drosselmeier, "on the contrary, what I have this time the honor to relate is droll and merry."

"Begin, begin then, dear Godfather!" cried the children, and the Counsellor began as follows.

THE STORY OF THE HARD NUT.

Pirlipat's mother was the wife of a king, and therefore a queen, and Pirlipat straightway at the moment of her birth a true princess. The king was beside himself with joy, when he saw his beautiful daughter, as she lay in the cradle. He shouted aloud, danced, jumped about upon one leg, and cried again and again, "Ha! ha! was there ever any thing seen more beautiful than my little Pirlipat?" Thereupon all the ministers, generals, presidents and staff officers jumped about upon one leg like the king, and cried aloud, "No, never!" And it was so, in truth, for as long as the world has been standing, a lovelier child was never born, than this

STORY OF THE "HARD NUT."

very Princess Pirlipat. Her little face seemed made of lilies and roses, delicate white and red; her eyes were of living sparkling azure, and it was charming to see how her little locks curled in bright golden ringlets. Besides this, Pirlipat had brought into the world two rows of little pearly teeth, with which two hours after her birth, she bit the high chancellor's finger, as he was examining her features too closely, so that he screamed out, "Oh, Gemini!" Others assert that he screamed out, "Oh, Crickee!" but on this point authorities are at the present day divided. Well, little Pirlipat bit the high chancellor's finger, and the enraptured land knew now that some sense dwelt in Pirlipat's beautiful body. As has been said, all were delighted. The queen alone was very anxious and uneasy, and no one knew wherefore, but every body remarked with surprise, the care with which she watched Pirlipat's cradle. Besides that the doors were guarded by soldiers, and not counting the two nurses, who always remained close by the cradle, six maids night after night sat in the room to watch. But what seemed very foolish, and no one could understand the meaning of it, was this; each of these six maids must have a cat upon her lap, and stroke it the whole night through, and thus keep it continually purring. It is impossible that you, dear children, can guess why Pirlipat's mother made all these arrangements, but I know, and will straightway tell you.

It happened that once upon a time many great kings and fine princes were assembled at the court of Pirlipat's father, on which occasion much splendor was displayed, the theatres were crowded, balls were given, and tournaments held almost every day. The king, in order to show plainly that he was in no want of gold and silver, was resolved to take a good handful out of his royal treasury, and expend it in a suitable manner. Therefore as soon as he had been privately informed by the overseer of the kitchen, that the court astronomer had predicted the right time for killing, he ordered a great feast of sausages, leaped into his carriage, and went himself to invite the assembled kings and princes to take a little soup with him, in order to enjoy the agreeable surprise which he had prepared for them. Upon his return, he said very affectionately to the queen, "You know, my dear, how extremely fond I am of sausages." The queen knew at once what he meant by that, and it was this, that she should take upon herself, as she had often done before, the useful occupation of making sausages. The lord treasurer must straightway bring to the kitchen the great golden sausage kettle, and the silver chopping knives and stew-pans. A large fire of sandal wood was made, the queen put on her damask apron, and soon the sweet smell of the sausage meat began to steam up out of the kettle. The agreeable odor penetrated even to the royal council chamber, and the king, seized with a sudden transport, could no longer restrain himself. "With your permission, my lords," he cried, and leaped up, ran as fast as he could into the kitchen, embraced the queen, stirred a little with his golden sceptre in the kettle, and then his emotion being quieted, returned calmly to the council.

The important moment had now arrived when the fat was to be chopped into little pieces, and browned gently in the silver stew-pans. The maids of honor now retired, for the queen, out of true devotion and reverence for her royal spouse, wished to perform this duty alone. But just as the fat began to fry, a small wimpering, whispering voice was heard, "Give me a little of the fat, sister—I should like my part of the feast—I too am a queen—give me a little of the fat." The queen knew very well that it was Lady Mouserings who said this. Lady Mouserings had lived these many years in the king's palace. She maintained that she was related to the royal family, and that she was herself a queen in the kingdom of Mousalia, for which reason she held a great court under the hearth. The queen was a kind and benevolent lady, and although she was not exactly willing to acknowledge Lady Mouserings as a true queen and sister, yet she was very ready to allow her a little banquet on this great holiday. She answered, therefore, "Come out, then, Lady Mouserings, you are welcome to a little of the fat." Upon this, Lady Mouserings leaped out very quickly and merrily, jumped upon the hearth, and seized with her dainty little paws, one piece of fat after the other as the queen reached it to her. But now, all the cousins and aunts of the Lady Mouserings came running out, besides her seven sons, rude and forward rogues, who all fell at once upon the fat, and the terrified queen could not drive them away. But as good fortune would have it, the chief maid of honor came in at this moment, and chased away the intruding guests, so that a little of the fat was left. The king's mathematician being summoned, demonstrated very clearly that there was enough remaining to season all the sausages, if distributed with the nicest judgment and skill.

Drums and trumpets were now heard without, and all the invited potentates and princes, some on white palfreys, some in crystal carriages, came in splendid apparel to the sausage-feast. The king received them kindly and graciously, and then, adorned with crown and sceptre, as became the monarch of the land, seated himself at the head of the table. Already in the first course, that of the sausage balls, it was observed that he grew pale and paler; raised his eyes to heaven; gentle sighs escaped from his bosom, and he seemed to undergo great inward suffering. But in the second course, which consisted of the long sausages, he sank back upon his throne, sobbing and moaning, held both hands to his face, and at last wept and groaned aloud. All sprang up from the table, the royal physician tried in vain to feel the pulse of the unhappy monarch, a deep-seated, unknown torture appeared to agitate him. At last, after much anxiety, and after the application of some very strong remedies, the king seemed to come a little to himself, and stammered out scarce audibly the words, "*Too little fat!*"

Then the queen threw herself in despair at his feet, and sobbed out, "Oh, my poor, unhappy, royal husband! Alas, how great must be the suffering which you endure! But see the guilty one at your feet; punish, punish her without mercy. Alas! Lady Mouserings with her seven sons, and aunts and cousins, *have eaten up the fat, and—*" with these words she fell right over backwards in a swoon. Then the king, full of rage, leaped up and cried out, "Chief maid of honor, how happened that?" The chief maid of honor told the story, as much as she knew of it, and the king resolved to take vengeance upon Lady Mouserings and her family for having eaten up the fat of his sausages. The privy council was called, and it was resolved to summon Lady Mouserings to trial, and confiscate all her estates. But as the king was of opinion that in the meanwhile she might eat up more of his sausage fat, the affair was placed at last in the hands of the royal watchmaker and mechanist.

This man (whose name was the same as mine, to wit, Christian Elias Drosselmeier) engaged, by means of a very singular and deep political scheme, to drive Lady Mouserings and her family from the palace forever. He invented therefore several curious little machines, in which a piece of toasted fat was fastened to a thread, and these Drosselmeier placed around lady Mouserings' dwelling. Lady Mouserings was much too wise not to see through Drosselmeier's craft, but all her warnings, all her entreaties were of no avail, every one of her seven sons, and many of her cousins and aunts, went into Drosselmeier's machines, and, as they tried to snap away the fat, were caught by an iron grating, which fell suddenly down behind them, and were afterwards miserably slaughtered in the kitchen. Lady Mouserings, with the little remnant of her family, forsook the dreadful place. Grief, despair, revenge filled her bosom. The court revelled in joy at this event, but the queen was very anxious, for she knew the disposition of Lady Mouserings, and was very sure that she would not suffer the death of her sons to go unavenged. In fact, Lady Mouserings appeared one day, when the queen was in the kitchen, preparing a harslet hash for her royal husband, a dish of which he was very fond, and said, "My sons, my cousins and aunts are destroyed; take care queen, that Mouse-Queen does not bite thy little princess in two—take good care." With this she disappeared, and was not seen again; but the queen was so frightened that she let the hash fall into the fire ; and thus a second time Lady Mouserings spoiled a favorite dish for the king, at which he was very angry.

"But this, dear children," said Drosselmeier, "is enough for to-night—the rest at another time."

Maria, who had her own thoughts about this story, begged Godfather Drosselmeier very hard to go on, but she could not prevail upon him. He rose, saying, "Too much at once is bad for the health—the rest to-morrow." As the Counsellor was just stepping out of the room, Fred called out, "Tell me, Godfather Drosselmeier, is it then really true that you invented mouse-traps ?"

"How can you ask such a silly question ?" said his mother, but the Counsellor smiled mysteriously, and said in an under tone, "Am I a skilful watchmaker, and yet not able to invent a mousetrap ?"

THE STORY OF THE HARD NUT CONTINUED.

You know now, children, commenced Counsellor Drosselmeier, on the following evening, why the queen took such care in guarding the beautiful Princess Pirlipat. Was it not to be feared that Lady Mouserings would execute her threat, that she would come again, and bite the little princess to death? Drosselmeier's machines were not the least protection against the wise and prudent Lady Mouserings, but the court astronomer, who was at the same time private star-gazer and fortune-teller to his majesty, declared it to be his opinion that the family of Baron Purr would be able to keep Lady Mouserings from the cradle. Most of that name were secretaries of legation at court, with little to do, though always at hand for an embassy to a foreign power, but they must now render themselves useful at home. And thus it came that each of the waiting-women must hold a son of that family upon her lap, and by continual and attentive fondling, lighten the severe public duties which fell to their lot.

Late one night the two chief nurses who sat close by the cradle, started up out of a deep sleep. All around lay in quiet slumber—no purring—the stillness of the grave! even the death-watch could be heard ticking! and what was the terror of the two chief waiting-women, as they just saw before them a large, dreadful mouse, which stood erect upon its hind feet, and had laid its ugly head close against the face of the princess. With a cry of terror they jumped up; all awoke, but in a moment Lady Mouserings (for the great mouse by Pirlipat's cradle was no one but she) ran as fast as she could to the corner of the chamber. The secretaries of legation leaped after her, but too late—she had disappeared through a hole in the chamber floor. Little Pirlipat awoke at the noise and wept bitterly. "Thank heaven," cried the nurse, "she lives—she lives!" But how great was their terror, when they looked at Pirlipat, and saw what a change had taken place in the sweet beautiful child. Instead of the white and red face with golden locks, a large, ill-shaped head sat upon her thin shrivelled body, her azure blue eyes were changed into green staring ones, and her little mouth had stretched itself from ear to ear. The queen was brought to death's door by grief and sorrow, and it was found necessary to hang the king's library with thick wadded tapestry, for again and again he ran his head against the wall, crying out at every time in lamentable tones, "Ah, me, unhappy monarch!" He might now have seen how much better it would have been to eat his sausages without fat, and to leave Lady Mouserings and her family at peace under the hearth; but Pirlipat's royal father did not think about this, he laid all the blame upon the court watchmaker and mechanist, Christian Elias Drosselmeier of Nuremburg. He therefore wisely decreed that Drosselmeier should restore the Princess Pirlipat to her former condition within four weeks, or at least find out some certain and infallible method of effecting this, otherwise he should suffer a shameful death under the axe of the executioner.

Drosselmeier was not a little terrified, but he had great confidence in his skill and good fortune, and began immediately the first operation which he thought useful. He took little Princess Pirlipat apart with great dexterity, unscrewed her little hands and feet, and carefully examined her inward structure; but he found, alas, that the princess would grow uglier as she grew bigger, and knew not what to do or what to advise. He put the princess carefully together again, and sank down by her cradle in despair, for he was not allowed to leave it. The fourth week had commenced—yes, Thursday had come, when the king looked in with flashing eyes, and shaking his sceptre at him, cried, "Christian Elias Drosselmeier, cure the princess, or thou must die." Drosselmeier began to weep bitterly, but the Princess Pirlipat lay as happy as the day, and cracked nuts. Pirlipat's uncommon appetite for nuts now occurred for the first time to the mechanist, and the fact likewise that she had come into the world with teeth.

In truth, immediately after her transformation, she had screamed continually until a nut accidentally came in her way, which she immediately put into her mouth, cracked it, ate the kernel, and then became quite composed. Since that time her nurses found that nothing pleased her so well as to be supplied with nuts. "Oh, sacred instinct of Nature! eternal, inexplicable sympathy of existence!" cried Christian Elias Drosselmeier. "Thou pointest me to the gates of this mystery. I will knock, and they will open." He begged straightway for permission to speak with the royal astronomer, and was led to his apartment under a strong guard. They embraced with many tears, for they had been warm friends, then retired into a private cabinet, and examined a great many books which treated of instinct, of sympathies, and antipathies, and other mysterious things. Night came on; the astronomer looked at the stars, and with the aid of Drosselmeier, who had great skill in such matters, set up the horoscope of Princess Pirlipat. It was a great deal of trouble, for the lines grew all the while more and more intricate; but at last —what joy!—at last it became clear, that the Princess Pirlipat, in order to be freed from the magic which had deformed her, and to regain her beauty, had nothing to do but to eat the kernel of the nut Crackatuck.

Now the nut Crackatuck had such a hard shell, that an eight-and-forty pounder might be wheeled over it without breaking it. This hard nut must be cracked with the teeth before the princess, by a man who had never been shaved, and had never worn boots. The young man must then hand her the kernel with closed eyes, and must not open them again until he had marched seven steps backward without stumbling. Drosselmeier and the astronomer had labored together, without cessation, for three days and nights, and the king was seated at dinner on Sunday afternoon, when the mechanist, who was to have been beheaded early Monday morning, rushed in with joy and transport, and proclaimed that he had found out a method of restoring to the Princess Pirlipat her lost beauty. The king embraced him with great kindness, and promised him a diamond sword, four orders of honor, and two new Sunday suits. "Immediately after dinner we will go to work," he added; "and see to it, dear mechanist, that the unshorn young man in shoes is ready at hand with the nut Crackatuck; and take care that he drinks no wine beforehand, for fear he should stumble as he goes the seven steps backward, like a crab; afterward he may drink like a fish." Drosselmeier was very much discomposed at these words; and, after much stuttering and stammering, said, that the method was discovered, indeed, but that the nut Crackatuck and the young man to crack it were yet to be sought after, and that it was quite doubtful whether nut or nutcracker would ever be found.

The king in great anger swung his sceptre about his crowned head, and roared with the voice of a lion, "Then off goes thy head!" It was very fortunate for the unhappy Drosselmeier, that the king's dinner had been cooked better than usual this day, so that he was in a pleasant humor, and disposed to listen to reason, while the good queen, who was moved by the hard fate of the mechanist, used her influence to soothe him. Drosselmeier then after a while took courage, and represented to the monarch, that he had performed his task in discovering the means to restore the princess to her beauty, and thus by the terms of the royal decree had secured his safety. The king said that was all trash, stupid stuff and nonsense, but resolved at last, that the watchmaker should leave the court instantly, accompanied by the royal astronomer, and never return without the nut Crackatuck in his pocket. By the intercession of the queen, he consented that the nutcracker might be summoned by a notice in all the home and foreign newspapers and journals.

Here the Counsellor broke off again, and promised to narrate the rest on the following evening.

CONCLUSION OF THE STORY OF THE HARD NUT.

The next evening as soon as the candles were lighted, Godfather Drosselmeier appeared, and continued his story as follows:

Drosselmeier and the astronomer had been fifteen years on their journey without seeing the least signs of the nut Crackatuck. It would take me a month, children, to tell where they went, and what strange things happened to them. I must pass them over, and commence where Drosselmeier sank at last into despondency, and felt a great desire to see his dear native city, Nuremburg. This desire came upon him all at once, as he was smoking a pipe of tobacco with his friend in the middle of a great wood in Asia. "Oh, sweet city," he cried, "sweet native city, sweet Nuremberg! He who has never seen thee, though he may have travelled to London, Paris, Rome, if his heart is not dead to emotion, must continually desire to visit thee—thee, oh Nuremberg, sweet city, where there are so many beautiful houses with windows!" As Drosselmeier grieved in such a sorrowful manner, the astronomer was moved with sympathy, and began to cry and howl so pitifully that it was heard far and wide through Asia. He soon composed himself again, wiped the tears out of his eyes, and said: "But why, my respected colleague, why sit here and howl? Why should we not go to Nuremberg? Is it not all the same, wherever we seek after this miserable nut, Crackatuck?"

"That is true," replied Drosselmeier, greatly consoled. Both arose, knocked out their pipes, and went straightforward out of the wood in the middle of Asia, right to Nuremburg. They had scarcely arrived there, when Drosselmeier ran to his brother, Christopher Zacharias Drosselmeier, puppet-maker, varnisher, and gilder, whom he had not seen for these many years. The watchmaker told him the whole story of the Princess Pirlipat, Lady Mouserings, and the nut Crackatuck, so that he struck his hands together, over and over again with astonishment, and exclaimed: "Ei, ei, brother, brother, what strange things are these!" Drosselmeier then related the history of his travels: how he had passed two years with King Date, how coldly he had been received by Prince Almond, and how he had sought information to no purpose of the Natural Society in Squirrelberg—in short, how his search everywhere had been in vain to find even the least signs of the nut Crackatuck.

During this account, Christopher Zacharias had often snapped his fingers, turned about on one foot, winked, laughed, clucked with his tongue, and then called out: "Hi—hem—ei—oh!—if it should!—" At last, he tossed his hat and wig up in the air, clasped his brother round the neck, and cried: "Brother, brother, you are safe!—safe, I say; for I must be wonderfully mistaken if I have not that nut Crackatuck at this very moment in my possession!" He then drew a little box from his pocket, and took out of it a gilded nut of moderate size. "See," he said, "this nut fell into my hands in this way. Many years ago, a stranger came here at Christmas time with a sack full of nuts, which he offered for sale cheap. Just as he passed my shop, he got into a quarrel with a nut-seller of this city, who did not like to see a stranger come hither to undersell him, and for this reason attacked him. The man put down his sack upon the ground, the better to defend himself, and at the same moment, a heavily-laden wagon passed directly over it; all the nuts were cracked in pieces except this one, which the stranger, with a singular smile, offered me, for a bright dollar of the year 1720. I thought that strange, but as I found in my pocket just such a dollar as the man wanted, I bought the nut, and gilded it over, without exactly knowing why I bought the nut so dear, or why I set so much store by it.

All doubt, whether this nut was actually the long-sought nut, Crackatuck, was instantly removed, when the astronomer was called, who carefully scraped off the gold, and found upon the rind the word Crackatuck, engraved in Chinese characters. The joy of the travellers was beyond bounds, and the brother the happiest man under the sun, for Drosselmeier assured him that his fortune was made, since he would have a considerable pension for the rest of his days, and then there was the gold which had been scraped off—he might keep that for gilding. The mechanist and the astronomer had both put on their night-caps, and were getting into bed as the latter commenced: "My worthy colleague, good fortune never comes single. Take my word for it, we have found, not only the nut Crackatuck, but also the young man who is to crack it, and hand the kernel to the princess. I mean nobody else than your brother's son. I cannot sleep; no, this very night I must cast the youth's horoscope." With these words, he threw the night-cap off his head, and began straightway to take an observation.

The brother's son was in truth a handsome, well grown young man, who had never been shaved, and who had never worn boots. In his early youth he had on Christmas nights gone around as a Merry Andrew, but this could not be seen in his behavior in the least, so well had his manners been formed by his father's care. On Christmas days he wore a handsome red coat trimmed with gold, a sword, a hat under his arm, and a curling wig. In this fine dress he would stand in his father's shop, and out of gallantry crack nuts for the young girls, for which reason he was called the handsome Nutcracker.

On the following morning the astronomer was in raptures; he fell upon the mechanist's neck, and cried, "It is he—we have him—he is found! But there are two things, worthy colleague, which we must see to. In the first place, we must braid for your excellent nephew a stout wooden queue, which shall be joined in such a way to his lower jaw, that it can move it with great force. In the next place, when we arrive at the king's palace, we must let no one know that we have brought the young man with us who is to crack the nut Crackatuck. It is best that he should not be found for a long time. I read in his horoscope, that after many young men have broken their teeth to no purpose, the king will promise to him who cracks the nut, and restores to the princess her lost beauty, the princess herself, and the succession to the throne as a reward."

His brother, the puppet-maker, was highly delighted to think that his son might marry the Princess Pirlipat, and become a prince and king, and he gave him up entirely into the hands of the two travellers. The queue which Drosselmeier fastened upon his young and hopeful nephew, answered admirably, so that he made a series of the most successful experiments, even upon the hardest peach-stones. As Drosselmeier and the astronomer had sent immediate information to the palace, of the discovery of the nut Crackatuck, suitable notices had been published, and when the travellers arrived, many handsome young men, and among them some handsome princes, had appeared, who trusting to their sound teeth, were ready to undertake the disenchantment of the princess. The travellers were not a little terrified when they beheld the princess again. Her little body, with its tiny hands and feet, was hardly able to carry her great misshapen head, and the ugliness of her face was increased by a white cotton beard, which had spread itself around her mouth, and over her chin. All happened as the astronomer had read in the horoscope. One youth in shoes after another, bit upon the nut Crackatuck until his teeth and jaws were sore, and as he was led away, half swooning, by the physician in attendance, sighed out, "That was a hard nut."

When the king, in the anguish of his heart, had promised his daughter and his kingdom to him who should effect the disenchantment, the handsome young Drosselmeier stepped forward, and begged for permission to begin the experiment. And no one had pleased the fancy of Princess Pirlipat as well as young Drosselmeier; she laid her little hand upon her heart, and sighed deeply, "Ah, if this might be the one who is to crack the nut Crackatuck, and become my husband!" After young Drosselmeier had gracefully saluted the king and queen, and then the Princess Pirlipat, he received the nut Crackatuck from the hands of the master of ceremonies, put it without hesitation between his teeth, pulled his queue very hard, and crack—crack—the shell broke into many pieces. He then nicely removed the little threads and broken bits of shell that hung to the kernel, and reached it with a low bow to the princess, after which he shut his eyes, and began to walk backwards. The princess straightway swallowed the kernel, and behold! her ugly shape was gone, and in

THE DISENCHANTMENT OF THE PRINCESS.

its place appeared a most beautiful figure, with a face of roses and lilies, delicate white and red, eyes of living, sparkling azure, and locks curling in bright golden ringlets.

Drums and trumpets mingled their sounds with the loud rejoicings of the people. The king and his whole court danced, as at Pirlipat's birth, upon one leg; and the queen had to be carefully tended with Cologne water, because she had fallen into a swoon from delight and rapture. Young Drosselmeier, who had still his seven steps to perform, was a good deal discomposed by the tumult, but he kept firm, and was just stretching back his right foot for the seventh step, when Lady Mouserings rose squeaking and squealing out of the floor; down came his foot upon her head, and he stumbled, so that he hardly kept himself from falling. Alas! what a hard fate! As quick as thought, the youth was changed to the former figure of the princess. His body became shrivelled up, and was hardly able to support his great misshapen head, his eyes turned green and staring, and his mouth was stretched from ear to ear. Instead of his queue, a narrow wooden cloak hung down upon his back, with which he moved his lower jaw.

The watchmaker and astronomer were benumbed with terror and affright, while Lady Mouserings rolled bleeding and kicking upon the floor. Her malice did not go unpunished, for young Drosselmeier had trodden upon her neck so heavily with the sharp heel of his shoe that she could not survive. When Lady Mouserings lay in her last agonies, she squeaked and whimpered in a piteous tone: "Oh, Crackatuck! hard nut—hi, hi!—of thee I now must die!—que, que—son with seven crowns will bite—Nutcracker—at night—hi, hi—que, que—and revenge his mother's death—short breath—must I—hi, hi—die, die—so young—que, que—oh, agony!—queek!" With this cry, Lady Mouserings died, and the royal oven-heater carried out her body. As for yonng Drosselmeier, no one troubled himself any further about him, but the princess put the king in mind of his promise, and he commanded that they should bring the young hero before him. But when the unfortunate youth approached, the princess held both hands before her face, and cried, "Away, away with the ugly Nutcracker!" The court marshal immediately took him by the shoulders, and pushed him out of doors. The king was full of anger, because they had wished to give him a Nutcracker for a son-in-law, and he put all the blame upon the mechanist and astronomer, and banished them forever from the kingdom. This did not stand in the horoscope which the astronomer had set up at Nuremberg, but he did not allow himself to be discouraged. He straightway took another observation, and declared that he could read in the stars, that young Drosselmeier would conduct himself so well in his new station, that in spite of his deformity, he would yet become a prince and a king; and that his former beauty would return, as soon as the son of Lady Mouserings, who had been born with seven heads, after the death of her seven sons, had fallen by his hand, and a maiden had loved him, notwithstanding his ugly shape. And they say that young Drosselmeier has actually been seen about Christmas time in his father's shop at Nuremberg, as a Nutcracker, it is true, but, at the same time, as a prince.

This, children, is the story of the Hard Nut; and you know now why people say so often, "That was a hard nut!" and whence it comes that Nutcrackers are so ugly.

The Counsellor thus concluded his narration. Maria thought that the Princess Pirlipat was an ill-natured, ungrateful thing; and Fred declared, that if Nutcracker were any thing of a man, he would not be long in settling matters with the Mouse-King, and would get his old shape again very soon.

THE UNCLE AND NEPHEW.

If any one of my good readers has ever had the misfortune to cut himself with glass, he knows how it hurts, and how long a time it takes to heal. Whenever Maria tried to get up, she felt very dizzy, and so it continued for a whole week, during which time she was obliged to remain in bed; but at last she became entirely well, and could play about the chamber as merrily as ever. Every thing in the glass case looked prettily, for the trees, flowers, and houses, and beautiful puppets, stood there as new and bright as ever. But, best of all, Maria found her dear Nutcracker again. He stood on the second shelf, and smiled upon her with a good, sound set of teeth. In the midst of all the pleasure which she felt in gazing at her favorite, a pang went through her heart, when she thought that

Godfather Drosselmeier's story had been nothing else but the history of the Nutcracker, and of his quarrel with Lady Mouserings and her son. She knew well enough that her Nutcracker could be none other than the young Drosselmeier of Nuremberg—Godfather Drosselmeier's agreeable, but now, alas! enchanted, nephew. For, that the skilful watchmaker at the court of Pirlipat's father was the Counsellor Drosselmeier himself, she did not doubt for an instant, even while he was telling the story.

"But why was it that your uncle did not help you?—why did he not help you?" complained Maria, as it became clearer and clearer to her mind, that in that battle which she saw, Nutcracker's crown and kingdom were at stake. "Were not all the other puppets subject to him, and is it not plain that the prophecy of the astronomer has been fulfilled, and that young Drosselmeier is prince and king of the puppets?" While the shrewd Maria explained and arranged all this so well in her mind, she believed, since she had seen Nutcracker and his vassals in life and motion, that they actually did live and move. But that was not so; every thing in the glass case remained stiff and lifeless; yet Maria, far from giving up her conviction, cast all the blame upon the magic of Lady Mouserings and her seven-headed son. "But, if you are not able to move, or to talk to me, dear Master Drosselmeier," she said aloud to the Nutcracker, "yet I know well enough that you understand me, and know what a good friend I am to you. You may depend upon my help, and I will beg of your uncle to bring his skill to your assistance, whenever you have need of it." Nutcracker remained still and motionless, but it seemed to Maria as if a gentle sigh was breathed in the glass case, so that the panes trembled, scarce audibly indeed, but with a strange, sweet tone; and a voice rang out, like a little bell: "Maria mine—I'll be thine—and thou mine—Maria mine!" Maria felt, in the cold shuddering that crept over her, a singular pleasure.

Twilight had come on; the doctor, with Godfather Drosselmeier, entered the sitting-room; and it was not long before Louise had arranged the tea-table, and all sat around, talking cheerfully of various things. Maria had very quietly taken her little arm-chair, and seated herself close at Godfather Drosselmeier's feet. During a moment when they were all silent, she looked up with her large blue eyes in the Counsellor's face, and said: "I know, dear Godfather Drosselmeier, that my Nutcracker is your nephew, the young Drosselmeier, of Nuremberg, and he has become a prince, or king rather, as your companion, the astronomer, foretold. All has turned out exactly so. You know now that he is at war with the son of Lady Mouserings—with the hateful Mouse-King. Why do you not help him?" Maria then related the whole course of the battle, just as she had seen it, and was often interrupted by the loud laughter of her mother and Louise. Fred and Drosselmeier only remained serious. "Where does the child get all this strange stuff in her head?" said the doctor.

"She has a lively imagination," replied the mother; "in fact, they are nothing but dreams caused by her violent fever."

"That story is not true," said Fred. "My red hussars are not such cowards as that. If I thought so—swords and daggers!—I would make a stir among them!"

But Godfather Drosselmeier, with a strange smile, took little Maria upon his lap, and said in a softer tone than he was ever heard to speak in before: "Ah, dear Maria, more power is given to thee than to me, or to the rest of us. Thou, like Pirlipat, art a princess born, for thou dost reign in a bright and beautiful kingdom. But thou hast much to suffer, if thou wouldst take the part of the poor misshapen Nutcracker, for the Mouse-King watches for him at every hole and corner. I cannot, thou—thou alone canst rescue him; be firm and true." Neither Maria nor any one else knew what Drosselmeier meant by these words; and they appeared so singular to Doctor Stahlbaum, that he felt the Counsellor's pulse, and said: "Worthy friend, you have some violent congestion about the head; I will prescribe something for you." But the mother shook her head thoughtfully, and spoke: "I feel what it is that the Counsellor means, but I cannot express it in words."

THE VICTORY.

Not long after, Maria was awaked one moonlight night by a strange rattling, that seemed to come out of a corner of the chamber. It sounded as if little stones were thrown and rolled about; and every now and then there was a terrible squeaking and squealing. "Ah! the mice—the mice are coming again!" exclaimed Maria, in affright; and she was about to wake her mother, but her voice failed her, and she could stir neither hand nor foot, for she saw the Mouse-King work his way out of a hole in the wall, then run, with sparkling eyes and crowns, around and around the chamber, when, at last, with a desperate leap, he sprang upon the little table that stood close by her bed. "Hi—hi—hi—must give me thy sugar-plums—thy ginger-bread—little thing—or I will bite thy Nut-cracker—thy Nutcracker!" So squeaked the Mouse-King, and snapped and grated hideously with his teeth, then sprang down again, and away through the hole in the wall. Maria was so distressed by this occurrence that she looked very pale in the morning, and was scarcely able to say a word. A hundred times she was going to inform her mother or Louise of what had happened, or at least to tell Fred, but she thought: "No one will believe me, and I shall only be laughed at." This, at least, was very clear, that if she wished to save little Nutcracker, she must give up her sugar-plums and her gingerbread. So, in the evening, she laid all that she had—and she had a great deal—down before the foot of the glass case.

The next morning, her mother said: "It is strange what brings the mice all at once into the sitting-room. See, poor Maria, they have eaten up all your gingerbread." And so it was. The ravenous Mouse-King had not found the sugar-plums exactly to his taste, but he had gnawed them with his sharp teeth, so that they had to be thrown away. Maria did not grieve about her cake and sugar-plums, for she was greatly delighted to think that she had saved little Nutcracker. But what was her terror, when the very next night she heard a squeaking and squealing close to her ear! Ah, the Mouse-King was there again, and his eyes sparkled more dreadfully, and he whistled and squeaked much louder than before: "Must give me thy sugar-puppets—chocolate figures—little thing—or I will bite thy Nutcracker—thy Nutcracker!" and with this, the terrible Mouse-King sprang down, and ran away again. Maria was very sad; she went the next morning to the glass case, and gazed with the most sorrowful looks at her sugar and chocolate figures. And her grief was reasonable, for thou canst not imagine, my attentive reader, what beautiful figures of sugar and chocolate little Maria Stahlbaum possessed. A pretty shepherd and shepherdess watched a whole flock of milk-white lambs, while a little dog frisked about them; next came two letter-carriers, with letters in their hands; and then four neat pairs of nicely-dressed boys and girls, with gay ribbons, rocked at see-saw upon as many boards, white and smooth as marble. Behind some dancers, stood Farmer Caraway and the Maid of Orleans—these Maria did not care so much about; but close in a corner stood her darling, a little red-cheeked baby, and now the tears came into her eyes. "Ah, dear Master Drosselmeier," she said, turning to Nutcracker, "there is nothing that I will not do to save you, but this is very hard!" Nutcracker looked all the while so sorrowfully, that Maria, who felt as if she saw the Mouse-King open his seven mouths, to devour the unhappy youth, resolved to sacrifice them all. So at evening, she placed all her sugar figures down at the foot of the glass case, just as she had done before with her sugar-plums and cake. She kissed the shepherd, and the shepherdess, and the lambs, and at last took her darling, the little red-cheeked baby out of the corner, and placed it down behind all the rest; Farmer Caraway and the Maid of Orleans must stand in the first row.

"Well, that is too bad!" said her mother, the next morning. "A mouse must have got into the glass case, for all poor Maria's sugar figures are gnawed and bitten in pieces." Maria could not keep from shedding tears, but she soon smiled again, and said to herself: "That is nothing, if Nutcracker is only saved." In the evening, her mother told the Counsellor of the mischief which the mouse had been doing in the glass case, and said: "It is provoking that we cannot destroy this fellow that makes such havoc with Maria's sugar toys."

"Ha!" cried Fred, merrily, "the baker opposite has a fine, gray secretary of legation; suppose I bring him over? He will soon make an end of the thing; he will have the mouse's head off, very quickly, even if it be Lady Mouserings herself, or her son, the Mouse-King."

"And jump about the tables and chairs," said his mother, laughing, "and throw down cups and saucers, and do all kinds of mischief."

"Ah, no indeed," said Fred; "the baker's secretary of legation is a light, careful fellow.

I wish I could walk on the roof of a house as well as he!"

"Let us have no cats in the night," said Louise, who could not bear them.

"Fred's plan is the best," said the doctor, but we will try a trap first. Have we got one?"

"Godfather Drosselmeier can make them best," said Fred, "for he invented them."

All laughed; and, when the mother said that there was no mouse-trap in the house, the Counsellor assured her that he had a number in his possession, and immediately sent for one. In a short time it was brought, and a very excellent mouse-trap it seemed to be. The story of the Hard Nut now came vividly to the minds of the children. As the cook toasted the fat, Maria shook and trembled. Her head was full of the story and its wonders, and she said to her old friend Dora: "Ah, great Queen, take care of Lady Mouserings and her family!" But Fred had drawn his sword, and cried: "Let them come on!—let them come on! I will scatter them!" But all remained still and quiet under the hearth. As the Counsellor tied the fat to a fine piece of thread, and set the trap softly, softly down by the glass case, Fred cried out: "Take care, Godfather Mechanist, or Mouse-King will play you a trick!"

Ah, but what a night did Maria pass! Something cold as ice tapped here and there against her arm; and crept, rough and hideous, upon her cheek, and squeaked and squealed in her ear. The hateful Mouse-King sat upon her shoulder. He opened his seven blood-red mouths, and, grating and snapping his teeth, he squeaked and hissed in her ear: "Wise mouse — wise mouse—goes not into the house—goes not to the feast—likes sugar things best—craft set at naught—will not be caught—give, give all—new frock—picture books—all the best—or shall have no rest.—I will tear and bite—Nutcracker at night—hi, hi—que, que!" Maria was full of sorrow and anxiety. She looked very pale and disturbed on the following morning, when Fred told her that the mouse had not been caught, so that her mother thought that she was grieving for her sugar things, or perhaps was afraid of the mouse. "Do not grieve, dear child," she said; "we will soon get rid of him. If the trap does not answer, Fred shall bring his gray secretary of legation."

As soon as Maria was alone in the sitting-room, she stepped to the glass case, and said, sobbing, to Nutcracker: "Ah, my dear, good Mr. Drosselmeier, what can I—poor, unhappy maiden—do? for, if I should give up all my picture-books, and even my new, beautiful frock, to the hateful mouse, he will ask more and more. And, when I have nothing left to give him, he will at last want me, instead of you, to bite in pieces." As little Maria grieved and sorrowed in this way, she observed a large spot of blood on Nutcracker's neck, which had been there ever since the battle. Now, after Maria had known that her Nutcracker was young Drosselmeier, the Counsellor's nephew, she did not carry him any more in her arms, nor hug and kiss him, as she used to do; indeed, she would very seldom move or touch him; but when she saw the spot of blood, she took him carefully from the shelf, and commenced rubbing it with her pocket-handkerchief. But what was her astonishment, when she felt that he suddenly grew warm in her hand, and began to move! She put him quickly back upon the shelf again, when—behold!—his little mouth began to work and twist, and move up and down, and at last, with a great deal of labor, he lisped out: "Ah, dearest, best Miss Stahlbaum—excellent friend, how shall I thank you? No! no picture-books, no Christmas frock!—Get me a sword—a sword. For the rest, I—" Here speech left him, and his eyes, which had begun to express the deepest sympathy, became staring and motionless.

Maria did not feel the least terror; on the contrary, she leaped for joy, for she had now found a way to rescue Nutcracker without any more painful sacrifices. But where should she obtain a sword for him? Maria at last resolved to ask advice of Fred; and in the evening, when their parents had gone out, and they sat alone together in the chamber by the glass case, she told him all that had happened to Nutcracker and Mouse-King, and then begged him to furnish the little fellow with a sword. Upon no part of this narration did Fred reflect so long and so earnestly as upon the poor account which she gave him of the bravery of his hussars. He asked once more very seriously, if it were so. Maria assured him of it upon her word, when Fred ran quickly to the glass case, addressed his hussars in a very moving speech, and then, as a punishment for their cowardice, cut their military badges from their caps, and forbade them for a year to play the Hussar's Grand March. After this, he turned again to Maria, and said: "As to a sword, I can easily supply the little fellow with one. I yesterday permitted an old colonel of the cuirassiers to retire upon a pension, and consequently he has no farther use for his fine sharp sabre." The aforesaid colonel was living on the pension which Fred had allowed him, in the farthest corner of the third shelf. He was brought out, his fine silver sabre taken from him, and buckled about Nutcracker.

Maria could scarcely get to sleep that night, she was so anxious and fearful. About midnight, it seemed to her as if she heard a strange rustling, and rattling, and slashing, in the sitting-room. All at once, it went "Queek!" "The Mouse-King!—the Mouse-King!" cried Maria, and sprang in her fright out of bed. All was still; but presently she heard a gentle knocking at the door, and a soft voice was heard: "Worthiest, best, kindest Miss Stahlbaum, open the door without fear—good tidings!"

Maria knew the voice of the young Drosselmeier, so she threw her frock about her, and opened the door. Little Nutcracker stood without, with a bloody sword in his right hand, and a wax taper in his left. As soon as he saw Maria, he bent down on one knee, and said: "You, oh lady—you alone it was, that filled me with knightly courage, and gave this arm strength to contend with the presumptuous foe who dared to disturb your slumber. The treacherous Mouse-King is overcome; he lies bathed in his blood. Scorn not to receive the tokens of victory from a knight who will remain devoted to your service until death." With these words, Nutcracker took off the seven crowns of the Mouse-King, which he had hung upon his left arm, and reached them to Maria, who received them with great joy. Nutcracker then arose, and said: "Best, kindest Miss Stahlbaum, you know not what beautiful things I could show you at this moment while my enemy lies vanquished, if you

NUT-CRACKER PROCLAIMS HIS VICTORY OVER MOUSE KING.

would have the condescension to follow me for a few steps. Oh, will you not be so kind? will you not be so good, best, kindest Miss Stahlbaum?"

THE PUPPET KINGDOM.

I BELIEVE that none of you, children, would have hesitated for an instant to follow the good, honest Nutcracker, who could never have meditated any evil. Maria consented to follow him, so much the more readily, because she knew what claims she had upon his gratitude, and because she was convinced that he would keep his word, and show her many beautiful things. "I will go with you, Master Drosselmeier," she said; "but it must not be far, and it must not be long, for as yet I have hardly had any sleep."

"I will choose, then," replied Nutcracker, the nearest, though a more difficult way." He went onward, and Maria followed him, until he stopped before a large, antique wardrobe, which stood in the hall. Maria perceived, to her astonishment, that the doors of this wardrobe, which were always kept locked, now stood wide open, so that she could see her father's fox-furred travelling coat, which hung in front. Nutcracker clambered very nimbly up by the carved figures and ornaments, until he could grasp the large tassel which hung down the back of the coat, and was fastened to it by a thick cord. As soon as Nutcracker pulled upon the tassel, a neat little stairs of cedar-wood stretched down from the sleeve of the travelling-coat to the floor. "Ascend, if you please, dearest Miss," cried Nutcracker. Maria did so; but scarcely had she gone up the sleeve—scarcely had she seen her way out at the collar, when a dazzling light broke forth upon her, and all at once she stood upon a sweet-smelling meadow, surrounded by millions of sparks, which darted up like flashing jewels. "We are now upon

Candy Meadow," said Nutcracker; "but we will directly pass through yonder gate." When Maria looked up, she saw the beautiful gate, which stood a few steps before them upon the meadow. It seemed built of variegated marble, of white, brown, and raisin color; but when Maria came nearer, she perceived that the whole mass consisted of sugar, almonds and raisins, kneaded and baked together, for which reason the gate, as Nutcracker assured her when they passed through it, was called the Almond and Raisin Gate. Upon a gallery built over the gate, made apparently of barley-sugar, there were six apes, in red jackets, who struck up the finest Turkish music which was ever heard, so that Maria scarcely observed that they were walking onward and onward, over a rich mosaic, which was nothing else than a pavement of nicely-inlaid lozenges. Very soon the sweetest odors streamed around them, which were wafted from a wonderful little wood, that opened on each side before them. There it shone and sparkled so, among the dark leaves, that the golden and silvery fruit could plainly be seen hanging from their gayly-colored stems, while the trunks and branches were ornamented with ribbons and nosegays; and when the orange perfume stirred and moved like a soft breeze, how it rustled among the boughs and leaves, and the golden fruit rocked and rattled in merry music, to which the bright, dancing sparkles kept time! "Ah, how delightful it is here!' cried Maria, entranced in happiness.

"We are in Christmas Wood, best miss," said Nutcracker.

"Ah, if I could but linger here a while," cried Maria. "Oh, it is too, too charming!"

Nutcracker clapped his hands, and some little shepherds and shepherdesses, and hunters and huntresses came near, who were so delicate and white, that they seemed made of pure sugar. They brought a dainty little arm-chair, all of gold, laid upon it a green cushion of candied citron, and invited Maria very politely to sit down. She did so, and immediately the shepherds and shepherdesses danced a very pretty ballet, while the hunters very obligingly blew their horns, and then all disappeared again in the bushes. "Pardon, pardon, kindest Miss Stahlbaum," said Nutcracker, "the dance was miserably performed, but the people all belong to our company of wire dancers, and they can do nothing but the same, same thing; they are deficient in variety. And the hunters blew so dull and lazily—but shall we not walk a little farther?"

"Ah, it was all very pretty, and pleased me very much," said Maria, as she rose, and followed Nutcracker.

They now walked along by a soft, rustling brook, out of which all the sweet perfumes seemed to arise which filled the whole wood. "This is the Orange Brook," said Nutcracker, "but its fine perfume excepted, it cannot compare either in size or beauty with Lemonade River, which like it empties into Orgeat Lake." In fact Maria very soon heard a louder rustling and dashing, and then beheld the broad Lemonade River, which rolled in proud cream-colored billows, between banks covered with bright green bushes. A refreshing coolness arose out of its noble waves.

Not far off, a dark yellow stream dragged itself lazily along, but it gave forth a very sweet odor, and a great number of little children sat on the shore angling for little fish, which they ate up as soon as caught. When Maria came nearer she observed that these fish were shaped almost like peanuts. At a distance there was a very neat little village, on the borders of this stream; houses, churches, parsonages, barns, were all dark brown, but many of the roofs were gilded, and some of the walls were painted so strangely, that it seemed as if little sugar-plums and bits of citron were stuck upon them. "That is Gingerbreadville," said Nutcracker, "which lies on Molasses River. Very pretty people live in it, but they are a little ill-tempered, because they suffer a good deal from the toothache, and so we will not visit it."

At this moment Maria observed a little town in which the houses were clear and transparent, and of different colors, which was a very pretty sight to look at. Nutcracker went straight forward towards it, and now Maria heard a busy, merry clatter, and saw a thousand tiny little figures, collected around some heavily laden wagons, which had stopped in the market. These they unloaded, and what they took out looked like sheets of colored paper and chocolate cakes. "We are now in Bonbon Town," said Nutcracker. "An importation has just arrived from Paper Land, and from King Chocolate. The poor people of Bonbon Town are often terribly threatened by the armies of Generals Fly and Gnat, for which reason they fortify their houses with stout materials from Paper Land, and throw up fortifications of the strong bulwarks, which King Chocolate sends to them. But, worthiest Miss Stahlbaum, we will not visit all the little towns and villages of this land. To the capital--to the capital!"

Nutcracker hastened forward, and Maria followed full of curiosity. It was not long before a sweet odor of roses enveloped them, and every thing around was touched with a soft rose-colored tint. Maria soon observed that this was the reflection of the red glancing lake, which rustled and danced before them, with charming and melodious tones in little rosy waves. Beautiful silver-white swans with golden collars, swam over the lake singing sweet tunes, while little diamond fish dipped up and down in the rosy water, as if in the merriest dance. "Ah," exclaimed Maria, ardently, "this is then the lake which Godfather Drosselmeier was once going to make for me, and I myself am the maiden, who is to fondle and caress the dear swans."

Nutcracker laughed in a scornful manner, such as Maria had never observed in him before, and then said: "Godfather Drosselmeier can never make any thing like this. You—you yourself, rather, sweetest Miss Stahlbaum—but we will not trouble our heads about that. Let us sail across the Rose Lake to the capital."

THE CAPITAL.

Nutcracker clapped his little hands together again, when the Rose Lake began to dash louder, the waves rolled higher, and Maria perceived a car of shells, covered with bright, sparkling, gay-colored jewels, moving toward them in the distance, drawn by two golden-scaled dolphins. Twelve of the loveliest little Moors, with caps and aprons braided of humming-bird's feathers, leaped upon the shore, and carried, first Maria, and then Nutcracker, with a soft, gliding step, over the waves, and placed them in the car, which straightway began to move across the lake. Ah, how delightful it was as Maria sailed along, with the rosy air and the rosy waves breathing and dashing around her! The two golden-scaled dolphins raised up their heads, and spouted clear, crystal streams out of their nostrils, high, high in the air, which fell down again in a thousand quivering, flashing rainbows, and it seemed as if two small silver voices sang out: "Who sails upon the rosy lake? The little fairy—awake, awake! Music and song—bim-bim, fishes—sim-sim, swans—tweet-tweet, birds—whiz-whiz, breezes!—rustling, ringing, singing, blowing!—a fairy o'er the waves is going! Rosy billows, murmuring, playing, dashing, cooling the air!—roll along, along."

But the singing of the falling fountains did not seem to please the twelve little Moors, who were seated up behind the car, for they shook their parasols so hard that the palm-leaves of which they were made rattled and clattered, and they stamped with their feet in very strange time, and sang, "Klapp and klipp, and klipp and klapp, backward and forward, up and down!" "Moors are a merry folk," said Nutcracker, somewhat disturbed," but they will make the whole lake rebellious." And very soon there arose a confused din of strange voices, which seemed to float in the sea and in the air; but Maria did not heed them, for she was gazing in the sweet-scented, rosy waves, out of which the face of a charming little maiden smiled up upon her. "Ah!" she cried joyfully, and struck her hands together. "Look, look, dear Master Drosselmeier! There is the Princess Pirlipat down in the water! Oh, how sweetly she smiles upon me!"

Nutcracker sighed quite sorrowfully, and said: "Oh, kindest Miss Stahlbaum, that is not the Princess Pirlipat—it is you, you—it is your own lovely face that smiles so sweetly out of the Rose Lake." Upon this, Maria drew her head back very quickly, put her hands before her face, and blushed very much. At this moment, she was lifted out of the car by the twelve Moors, and carried to the shore. They now found themselves in a little thicket, which was perhaps more beautiful even than the Christmas Wood, it was so bright and sparkling. What was most wonderful in it were the strange fruits that hung upon the trees, which were not only curiously colored, but gave out also every kind of sweet odor. "We are in Sweetmeat Grove," said Nutcracker, "but yonder is the Capital."

And what a sight! How can I venture, children, to describe the beauty and splendor of the city which now displayed itself to Maria's eyes, upon the broad, flowery meadow before them? Not only did the walls and towers glitter with the gayest colors, but the style of the buildings was like nothing else that is to be found in the world. Instead of roofs, the houses had diadems set upon them, braided and twisted in the daintiest manner; and the towers were crowned with variegated trellis-work, and hung with festoons the most beautiful that ever were seen. As they passed through the gate, which looked as if it were built of macaroons and candied fruits, silver soldiers presented arms, and a little man in a brocade dressing-gown threw himself upon Nutcracker's neck, with the words: "Welcome, best prince! welcome to Confectionville!"

Maria was not a little astonished to hear young Drosselmeier called a prince by such a distinguished man. But she now heard such a hubbub of little voices, such a huzzaing and laughter, such a singing and playing, that she could think of nothing else, and turned to Nutcracker to ask him what it all meant. "Oh, worthiest Miss Stahlbaum, it is nothing uncommon. Confectionville is a populous and merry city; thus it goes here every day. Let us walk farther, if you please."

They had only gone a few steps, when they came to the great market-place, which presented a wonderful sight. All the houses around were of sugared filagree work; gallery was built over gallery, and in the middle stood a tall obelisk of white and red sugared cream, while four curious, sweet fountains played in the air, of orgeat, lemonade, mead, and soda-water, and in the great basin were soft bruised fruits, mixed with sugar and cream, and touched a little by the frost.

But prettier than all this were the charming little people, who, by thousands, pushed and squeezed, knocked their heads together, huzzaed, laughed, jested, and sang—who had raised indeed that merry din which Maria had heard at a distance. Here were beautifully-dressed men and women, Armenians and Greeks, Jews and

Tyrolese, officers and soldiers, preachers, shepherds, and harlequins—in short, all the people that can possibly be found in the world. On one corner the tumult increased; the people rocked and reeled to clear the way, for just at that moment the Grand Mogul was carried by in a palanquin, attended by ninety-three grandees of the kingdom, and seven hundred slaves. Now, on the opposite corner, the fishermen, five hundred strong, were marching in procession; and it happened, very unfortunately, that the Grand Turk took it into his head just then to ride over the market-place with three thousand Janissaries, besides which a long train came from the Festival of Sacrifices, with sounding music, singing: "Up, and thank the mighty sun!" and pushed straight on for the obelisk. Then what a squeezing, and a pushing, and a rattling, and a clattering. By and by, a screaming was heard, for a fisherman had knocked off a Brahmin's head in the crowd, and the Great Mogul was almost run over by a Harlequin. The tumult grew wilder and wilder, and they had commenced to beat and strike each other, when the man in the brocade dressing-gown, who had called Nutcracker a prince at the gate, clambered up by the obelisk, and having thrice pulled a little bell, called out three times: "Confiseur! confiseur! confiseur!"

The tumult was immediately appeased; each one tried to help himself as well as he could; and, after the confused trains and processions were set in order, and the dirt upon the Great Mogul's clothes was brushed off, and the Brahmin's head put on again, the former hubbub began anew. "What do they mean by 'Confiseur,' good Master Drosselmeier?" asked Maria.

"Ah, best Miss Stahlbaum," replied Nutcracker, "by 'Confiseur' is meant an unknown but very fearful power, which they believe can do with them as he pleases; it is the Fate that rules over this merry little people, and they fear it so much, that the mere mention of the name is able to still the greatest tumult. Each one then thinks no longer of any thing earthly—of cuffs, and kicks, and broken heads, but retires within himself, and says: 'What are we, and what is our destiny?'"

Maria could not refrain from a loud exclamation of surprise and wonder, as all at once they stood before a castle glimmering with rosy light, and crowned with a hundred airy towers. Beautiful nosegays of violets, narcissuses, tulips, and dahlias, were hung about the walls, and their dark, glowing colors only heightened the dazzling, rose-tinted, white ground upon which they were fastened. The large cupola of the centre building and the sloping roofs of the towers were spangled with a thousand gold and silver stars. "We are now in front of Marchpane Castle," said Nutcracker. Maria was completely lost in admiration of this magic palace, yet it did not escape her that one of the large towers was without a roof, while little men were moving around it upon a scaffolding of cinnamon, as if busied in repairing it. But before she had time to inquire about it, Nutcracker continued: "Not long ago, this beautiful castle was threatened with serious injury, if not with entire destruction. The Giant Sweet-tooth came this way, and bit off the roof of yonder tower, and was gnawing upon the great cupola, when the people of Confectionville gave up to him a full quarter of the city, and a considerable portion of Sweetmeat Grove, as tribute, with which he contented himself, and went his way."

At this moment soft music was heard, the doors of the palace opened, and twelve little pages marched out with lighted cloves, which they carried in their hands like torches. Each of their heads was a pearl; their bodies were made of rubies and emeralds; and they walked upon feet cast out of pure gold. Four ladies followed them, almost as tall as Maria's Clara, but so richly and splendidly dressed, that she saw in a moment that they were princesses born. They embraced Nutcracker in the tenderest manner, and cried with joyful sobs: "Oh, my prince, my best prince! Oh, my brother!"

Nutcracker seemed very much moved; he wiped the tears out of his eyes; then took Maria by the hand, and said with great emotion: "This is Miss Maria Stahlbaum, the daughter of a much-respected and very worthy physician, and she is the preserver of my life. Had she not thrown her shoe at the right time—had she not supplied me with the sword of a pensioned colonel, I should now be lying in my grave, torn and bitten to pieces by the terrible Mouse-King. View her—gaze upon her, and tell me, if Pirlipat, although a princess by birth, can compare with her in beauty, goodness, and virtue? No, I say no!"

And all the ladies cried out "No!" and then fell upon Maria's neck, exclaiming: "Ah, dear preserver of the prince, our beloved brother! charming Miss Maria Stahlbaum!" She now accompanied these ladies and Nutcracker into the castle, and entered a room, the walls of which were of bright, colored crystal. But of all the beautiful things which Maria saw here, what pleased her most were the nice little chairs, sofas, secretaries, and bureaus, with which the room was furnished, and which were all made of cedar or Brazil-wood, and ornamented with golden flowers. The princesses made Maria and Nutcracker sit down, and said that they would immediately prepare something for them to eat. They then brought out a great many little cups and saucers, and plates and dishes, all of the finest porcelain, and spoons, knives, and forks, graters, kettles, pans, and other kitchen furniture, all of gold and silver.

Then they brought the finest fruits and sugar-things, such as Maria had never seen before, and began in the nicest manner to squeeze the fruits with their little snow-white hands, and to pound the spice, and grate the sugar-almonds, in short, so to turn and handle every thing, that Maria could see how well the princesses had been brought up, and what a delicious meal they were preparing. As she desired very much to learn sŭch things, she could not help wishing to herself that she might assist the princesses in their labor. The most beautiful of Nutcracker's sisters, as if she had guessed Maria's secret thoughts, reached her a little golden mortar, saying: "Oh, sweet friend, dear preserver of my brother, will you not pound a little of this sugar-candy?"

While Maria pounded in the mortar, Nutcracker began to give a full account of his adventures, of the dreadful battle between his army and that of the Mouse-King, and how he had lost it by the cowardice of his troops; how the terrible Mouse-King lay in wait to bite him in pieces, and how Maria, to preserve him, gave up many of his subjects, who had entered her service, and all just as it had happened. During this narration, it seemed to Maria, as if his words became less and less audible, and the pounding of her mortar also sounded more and more distant, until she could scarcely hear it; presently, she saw a silver gauze before her, in which the princesses, the pages, Nutcracker, and herself, too, were all enveloped. A singular humming, and rustling, and singing was heard, which seemed to die away in the distance; and now Maria was raised up, as if upon mounting waves, higher and higher—higher and higher—higher and higher!

THE CONCLUSION.

Prr—puff it went! Maria fell down from an immeasurable height. That was a fall! But she opened her eyes, and there she lay upon her little bed; it was bright day, and her mother stood by her, saying: "How can you sleep so long? breakfast has been ready this great while." You now perceive, kind readers and listeners, that Maria, completely confused by the wonderful things which she had seen, had at last fallen asleep in the room at Marchpane Castle, and that the Moors, or the pages, or perhaps even the princesses themselves must have carried her home, and laid her softly in bed. "Oh, mother, dear mother, you cannot think where young Master Drosselmeier led me last night, and what beautiful things I have seen!" And then she began and told the whole, almost as accurately as I have related it, while her mother listened in astonishment.

When she had finished, her mother said: "You have had a long and very beautiful dream, but now drive it all out of your head." Maria insisted upon it that she had not dreamed, but had actually seen what she had related, when her mother led her into the sitting-room, to the glass case; took Nutcracker out, who was standing, as usual, upon the second shelf, and said: "Silly child, how can you believe that this wooden Nuremberg puppet can have life or motion?"

"But, dear mother," replied Maria, "I know little Nutcracker is young Master Drosselmeier, of Nuremberg, Godfather Drosselmeier's nephew." Then her father and mother both laughed very heartily. "Ah, dear father," said Maria, almost crying, "you should not laugh so at my Nutcracker; he has spoken very well of you; for when we entered Marchpane Castle, and he presented me to his sisters, the princesses, he said that you were a much respected and very worthy physician." At this the laughter was still louder, and Louise, and even Fred, joined in. Maria then ran into the other chamber, took the seven crowns of the Mouse-King out of her little box, brought them in, and handed them to her mother, saying: "See here, dear mother, here are the seven crowns of the Mouse-King, which young Master Drosselmeier gave me last night, as a token of his victory." Her mother examined the little crowns in great astonishment; they were made of a strange but very shining metal, and were so delicately worked, that it seemed impossible that mortal hands could have formed them. Her father, likewise, could not gaze enough at them, and he insisted very seriously that Maria should confess how she obtained them. But she could give no other account of them, and kept firm to what she had said; and, as her father spoke very harshly to her, and even called her a little story-teller, she began to cry bitterly, and said: "Oh, what, what then shall I say?"

At this moment the door opened. The Counsellor entered, and exclaimed: "What's this? what's this?" The doctor told him of all that had happened, and showed him the little crowns. As soon as the Counsellor cast his eyes on them, he laughed and cried: "Stupid pack—stupid pack! These are the very crowns which I used to wear on my watch-chain, years ago, and which I gave to little Maria, on her birthday, when she was two years old. Don't you remember them?" Neither father nor mother could remember them; but when Maria saw that her parents had forgotten their anger, she ran to Godfather Drosselmeier, and said: "Ah, you know all about it, Godfather Drosselmeier. Tell them yourself, that my Nutcracker is your nephew, young Master Drosselmeier, of Nurem-berg, and that it was he who gave me the crowns!"

The Counsellor's face turned very dark and grave, and he muttered: "Stupid pack—stupid pack!" Upon this, the doctor took little Maria upon his knee, and said very seriously: "Listen to me, Maria. Once for all, drive your foolish dreams and nonsense out of your head. If I ever hear you say again, that the silly, ugly Nutcracker is the nephew of your Godfather Drosselmeier, I will throw him out of the window, and all the rest of your puppets, Miss Clara not excepted."

Poor Maria durst not now speak of all these wonders, but she thought so much the more. Her whole soul was full of them; for you may imagine, that things so fine and beautiful as those which she had seen are not easily forgotten. Even Fred turned his back upon his sister, whenever she spoke of the wonderful kingdom in which she had been so happy; and, it is said, that he sometimes would mutter between his teeth: "Silly goose!" But that I can hardly believe of so amiable and good-natured a fellow. This is certain, however, he no longer believed a word of what Maria had told him. He made a formal apology to his hussars, on public parade, for the injustice which he had done them; stuck in their caps feathers of goose-quill, much finer and taller than those of which they had been deprived; and permitted them again to blow the Hussar's Grand March. Ah, ha! we know best how it stood with their courage, when those hateful balls spotted their red coats!

Maria was not allowed, then, to speak any more of her adventures, but the images of that wonderful fairy kingdom played about her in sweet, rustling tones. She could bring them all back again, whenever she fixed her thoughts steadfastly upon them, and hence it came, that, instead of playing, as she formerly did, she would sit silent and thoughtful, musing within herself, for which reason the rest would often scold her, and call her a little dreamer. Some time after this, it happened that the Counsellor was busy, repairing a clock in Doctor Stahlbaum's house. Maria sat close by the glass case, and, lost in her dreams, was gazing at Nutcracker, when the words broke from her lips involuntarily: "Ah, dear Master Drosselmeier, if you actually were living, I would not behave like Princess Pirlipat, and slight you, because for my sake you had ceased to be a handsome young man!"

At this, the Counsellor screamed: "Hey—hey—stupid pack!" Then there was a clap, and a knock, so loud, that Maria sank from her chair in a swoon. When she came to herself, her mother was busied about her, and said: "How came such a great girl to fall from her chair? Here is Godfather Drosselmeier's nephew, just arrived from Nuremberg! Come—behave like a little woman!"

She looked up; the Counsellor had put on his glass wig again, and his brown coat; he was smiling very pleasantly, and he held by the hand a little but very well-shaped young man. His face was as white as milk, and as red as blood; he wore a handsome red coat, trimmed with gold, and shoes and white silk stockings; in his button-hole was stuck a nosegay; his hair was nicely powdered and curled; and down his back there hung a magnificent queue. The sword by his side seemed to be made of nothing but jewels, it flashed and sparkled so brightly, and the little hat which he carried under his arm looked as if it were overlaid with soft, silken flakes. It very soon appeared how polite and well-bred the young man was, for he had brought Maria a great many handsome playthings—the nicest gingerbread, and the same sugar figures which the Mouse-King had bitten to pieces; and for Fred he had brought a splendid sabre. At table, the little fellow cracked nuts for the whole company—the hardest could not resist him; with the right hand he put them in his mouth; with the left, he pulled hard upon his queue, and—crack—the nut fell in pieces! Maria had turned very red when she first saw the handsome young man; and she became still redder, when, after dinner, young Drosselmeier invited her to go with him into the sitting-room to the glass case.

"Play prettily together, children; I have nothing against it, since all my clocks are going," cried the Counsellor.

Scarcely was Maria alone with young Drosselmeier, when he stooped upon one knee, and said: "Oh, my very best Miss Stahlbaum, you see here at your feet the happy Drosselmeier, whose life you saved on this very spot. You said most amiably, that you would not slight me, like the hateful Princess Pirlipat, if I had become ugly for your sake. From that moment, I ceased to be a miserable Nutcracker, and resumed again my old—and, I hope, not disagreeable—figure. Oh, excellent Miss Stahlbaum, make me happy with your dear hand; share with me crown and kingdom; rule with me in Marchpane Castle, for there I am still king!"

Maria raised the youth, and said softly: "Dear Master Drosselmeier, you are a kind, good-natured young man; and, since you rule in such a charming land, among such pretty, merry people, I will be your bride." With this, Maria immediately became Drosselmeier's betrothed bride.

After a year and a day, he came, as I have heard, and carried her away in a golden chariot, drawn by silver horses. There danced at the wedding two-and-twenty thousand of the most splendid figures, adorned with pearls and diamonds; and Maria, it is said, is at this hour queen of a land, where sparkling Christmas woods, transparent Marchpane Castles—in short, where the most beautiful, the most wonderful things can be seen by those who will only have eyes for them.

THE END.